# The Clue at Price's Creek

*A North Carolina Lighthouse Adventure*

By M.C. Tillson

Illustrated by Lisa T. Bailey

*For Lexie, Gatlin, and Adam*
*who are part of the magic now.*

## The Clue at Price's Creek

ISBN 978-0-9764824-8-2

### A Lighthouse Adventure Book

Published by A&M Writing and Publishing
Santa Clara, California
www.amwriting.com

Printed in the U.S.A.
First printing, May 2015

# Contents

Can You Keep a Secret?  v

Chapter 1: Arrgh, Pirates!  11

Chapter 2: Arrgh, Sam!  19

Chapter 3: Ferry Tales  27

Chapter 4: Stede's Ending  37

Chapter 5: Hunting Scavengers  41

Chapter 6: Shadow Watching  47

Chapter 7: A Whale of a Tale  53

Chapter 8: Crossed Words  63

Chapter 9: Hills, Thrills, and Chills  69

Chapter 10: Rerouting  75

Chapter 11: Museum@Southport  81

Chapter 12: An Ill Wind  85

Chapter 13: All Aboard  97

Chapter 14: Homemade Vanilla  105

Chapter 15: On the Beach  111

Chapter 16: There Be Pirates  121

Check It Out  125

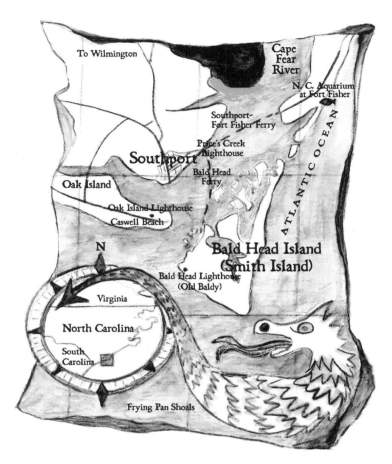

North Carolina has three capes on its shores: Cape Lookout, Cape Hatteras, and Cape Fear.

A cape is a large piece of land that sticks out into the sea—a little bit like a peninsula. However, a cape usually tells you that there's going to be a change in the coastline.

For example, when you travel north and go around Cape Fear, the shoreline changes: it extends farther out into the ocean and the water is shallow and rough. There are also shifting sandbars that can be extremely dangerous to passing ships. Cape Fear marks the beginning of the area known as the "Graveyard of the Atlantic."

iv

# Can You Keep a Secret?

It's not *that* big of a deal, but I don't tell just everybody because people will think I'm old fashioned (and maybe I am). But here's the thing: I love maps.

Don't get me wrong. I also like the cool GPS stuff and the talking directions that tell you where you are and where you're going and where the nearest ice-cream store is, but maps? Maps tell stories.

When I was about your age, my family took driving trips to lots of places. We drove to Tennessee to see my grandparents and to Raleigh, North Carolina, to see my aunt, uncle, and cousins. We drove to the Great Smoky Mountains and to the beach. On all of these trips, I looked at maps to see where we were going.

Maps tell you so much more than how to get somewhere. When you read about a place you've never been—or even when you read about a place you already know—maps help you understand that place better.

If you're traveling by car, maps give you information about the land you're crossing—like where the rivers and railroad tracks are. Maps can also help you figure out how long the trip will take. Those tiny numbers beside the roads on a map tell you how many miles there are between the markers—did you know that? (Just

add up the numbers to see how many miles you have to go.)

## Where Are We Now?

If this is your first North Carolina Lighthouse Adventure, you might want to know a couple of things. First of all, Sam and Becky—with their mom and dad—are on vacation with the Jamison family on North Carolina's Oak Island. Mom and Dad are still writing their book about lighthouses, and they visit as many as they can. Sam and Becky tag along because—well, because they don't have a choice, but also because some pretty interesting things can happen around lighthouses.

The other thing you should know is that Sam and Becky are in the middle of solving a mystery with their new friends, Troy, Andrew, and L.C. The mystery started with the pirate, Stede Bonnet—actually with the *ghost* of Stede Bonnet.

Becky, Sam, and their friends think Stede Bonnet's ghost needs help finding his lost treasure, but they aren't the only ones looking for it. The ghost of another pirate seems to be following them. Maybe you've heard of him? His name is Edward Teach, but people called him Blackbeard and he was one of the meanest pirates ever.

Is it just a coincidence that a man with gray-almost-white hair and a totally black beard started talking with Sam, Becky, Andrew, and Troy when they were crossing the Cape Fear River on the ferry?

The man seemed to know a lot about the area. During the ferry ride, he even pointed out the place where you can see three lighthouses at the same time: the Oak Island Lighthouse, the Bald Head Island Lighthouse, and—if you look very carefully toward the Southport side of the river—the abandoned Price's Creek Lighthouse. Sounds a little magical to me, don't you think? I wonder if that poem was magic too.

## Help with the Hard Words

When you choose what you want to read, I hope you pick some things with **unfamiliar** words. That's one of the best ways to learn! Most of the time you can figure out what a word means by looking at the other words or phrases around it. That's called the context of the word. But sometimes the context isn't there. Does that mean you should skip the word? I hope you don't!

**unfamiliar**
(un-fah-MILL-yur)
New or not well known.

When you're reading a Lighthouse Adventure Book and you see a word in bold, look on that same page for the meaning of the word and how to say it.

## Fact or Fiction?

You probably know that Sam and Becky and their friends and family are not real people. This is a fictional story, and they are characters from my imagination. However, the places I describe, and the historical people and events—including Stede Bonnet—are real parts of North Carolina history.

## Read More

There are lots of great books, websites, and other resources about North Carolina's Cape Fear, lighthouses, and pirates. A few of my favorites are at the end of this book. Want more? Just ask your librarian for help.

What? You don't have a librarian? Well you better find one fast! Everybody needs at least one librarian they can talk to. (You can thank me later!)

## Chapter 1
# Arrgh, Pirates!

"Hey, Dad. I have a question for you."

Sam clutched the side of the 180-foot boat that carried his friends and family across North Carolina's Cape Fear River. It was August and the afternoon temperature was creeping toward 100 degrees. The strong breeze that was making **whitecaps** on the water was a welcome relief.

**whitecaps**

(WHYT-kaps)
Waves that let you know there is wind or rough water. When waves are tall enough to fold (or "break") on themselves, they make foam that looks like white hats on the water. It takes winds of about 13 miles per hour to make whitecaps.

"Ask away," said Dad.

"What color was Blackbeard's beard?" said Sam.

"Is this some sort of a trick question, Sam?" Dad narrowed his eyes.

"What do you mean?" Sam was puzzled.

"Well, you're asking the color of Blackbeard's beard? Isn't that a bit like asking, 'Why did the chicken cross the road? or 'When is a door not a door?'"

Sam shook his head. "I still don't get it."

"Those are trick questions because they're the start of a riddle or joke," said Becky, Sam's older sister.

Becky stood beside Sam at the rail of the ferry. She kept an eye on the seagulls flying behind the boat as she tried to explain Dad's question. "A door isn't a door if it's **ajar**," she said. "A *jar*. Get it?"

**ajar**
(a-JAR)
Slightly open.
If you don't close a door entirely, the door is ajar.

"As for the chicken," she continued, "the answer *I've* always heard is that the chicken crossed the road to get to the other side."

Sam and Becky's new friend Andrew added, "Some people call them trick questions because the answer is too obvious and not really that funny. Sometimes the answer is a pun or uses a word that has two meanings. That can be funny—sometimes."

He smiled at Dad, "Have you heard the one that goes 'Why did the rubber chicken cross the road?'"

"To stretch its legs," answered Dad quickly. "See? That's what I'm talking about. It's the same sort of question as 'What color is Blackbeard's beard?'"

"Sounds like a trick question to me," said Mr. Jamison coming up behind Dad. "Like that riddle about the door being a jar, right?"

"Exactly," said Dad, "and I'm not falling for it."

Sam, Becky, Andrew, and Troy all rolled their eyes at the same time.

Mr. Jamison nodded wisely at Dad. "Don't worry, Mike. I'll handle this." He rubbed his chin thoughtfully and then looked sharply at Sam.

"Watch out, Sam," Andrew whispered. "My dad can be pretty tricky himself."

"Sam," said Mr. Jamison softly, "what color do *you* think Blackbeard's beard is?"

"Black," answered Sam promptly.

"Then why did you ask your Dad?"

"Because I didn't know if Blackbeard's beard would still be black if his hair was all gray. And I figured that Dad knew more than I did about gray hair because he's got so much."

**snickered**
(SNIK-erd)
Laughed quietly or laughed while trying to keep anyone else from noticing.

Mr. Jamison **snickered** at the look on Dad's face and took a big gulp of water to hide his smile.

Troy chimed in, "Right! And if we needed to know anything about bald heads, we'd ask *you*, Dad."

Mr. Jamison choked, and his big gulp of water spewed everywhere!

"Thanks, son," said Mr. Jamison as he wiped his face with his handkerchief. "I'm

glad you think of me as a good resource."
He frowned at Dad, who was holding his
stomach and laughing.

"To answer your question, Sam," said Mr.
Jamison, **deliberately**
turning his back on Dad,
"I assume the color of
Blackbeard's beard is
black. But, I also assume
that if he had lived to be older, both his
beard and his hair would have turned gray."

**✳deliberately**
(duh-LI-ber-ut-lee)
Doing something
on purpose or very
carefully.

Andrew jumped in and joined the
conversation. "But have you ever seen a guy
with all gray—almost white—hair and a
totally black beard with no gray in it at all?"

Mr. Jamison shook his head. "No, but I'm
sure it's possible."

"Dad, did you see anybody who looked
like that when we got on the ferry?" asked
Becky.

"Yeah, Dad," said Sam. "Did you see him? He was talking to us after the ferry left the dock."

"I didn't see you all talking to anybody except each other," said Mr. Jamison, looking around. "Can you point him out?"

"I…uh…I don't think he's on the ferry anymore," said Sam.

Dad snorted. "Not on the ferry? We're in the middle of the Cape Fear River, Sam! Where else would he be? Unless, of course, he's one of your ghost friends. Come on, Ed. Your shirt's still wet. Let's find you a towel."

## Chapter 2
# Arrgh, Sam!

Becky watched until the dads were out of **earshot**, and then she turned to Sam in disbelief.

"Really, Sam? 'What color was Blackbeard's beard?'" Becky shook her head. "I can't believe you did that! Why didn't you just say, 'Hi, Dad. Did you see that old guy talking to us? We think he might be the ghost of Blackbeard and we're pretty sure he's trying to keep us from finding Steed Bonnet's pirate treasure.

**earshot** ✳
(EER-shot)
How far away a voice can be heard. When someone is out of earshot, they can't hear you talking.

Why do we think that? Well, because the ghost of **Stede Bonnet** told us.'"

Becky shook her head. "Good job, Sam!" she said sarcastically.

"I don't know why I did that," said Sam. "I thought he knew something about Blackbeard—something that would help us figure out who that guy was. Do you have a better idea?"

Becky leaned on the rail beside Troy and Andrew. No one spoke as they watched the swarming seagulls fighting each other for bits of food.

Troy broke the silence. "I wonder if L.C.'s grandmother is home yet?"

## Stede Bonnet

Steed BON-it) Nicknamed "The Gentleman Pirate," Stede Bonnet decided to become a pirate in 1717. He bought a ship, loaded up his library of books, and began pirating along North Carolina's Cape Fear. Bonnet sank ships, stole cargo, and even made some of his captives "walk the plank." He had been a pirate only a few months when Blackbeard kidnapped him and took over his ship. About a year after Bonnet first became a pirate, soldiers captured him near Price's Creek. He was taken to prison in South Carolina and later hanged.

L.C. (whose real name is Lila Cunningham) lives on Oak Island with her grandmother. She's graduating from high school next year and going to college—if she can afford it. She's been saving her money and works as many jobs as she can— at the library, at the Southport museum, and even at the ice-cream store. (That's where Sam, Becky, Troy, and Andrew found her.)

The kids had received very odd messages at the Oak Island Lighthouse and on the beach below. The messages led them to L.C. (who had been getting her own mysterious messages) and to a trunk in her grandmother's attic.

Unfortunately, at the moment, the attic is locked. Fortunately, L.C.'s grandmother has the key. Unfortunately, L.C.'s grandmother has been out of town.

"What you really want to know," corrected Andrew, "is whether L.C. found the trunk that belonged to Stede Bonnet."

"Right," said Becky, "and if she did find it, did she open it."

"And," added Sam, "if her grandmother *is* back and if L.C. *did* find the trunk and if she *did* open it, then you want to know if there was anything in it, like—oh, I don't know— like pirate treasure?"

Troy sighed. "You're right. L.C. said her grandmother was coming home the day after tomorrow, and that was the day before yesterday, so that means today, right?"

Becky laughed. "Troy, I need a calendar and a calculator to figure out what you just said! But I think you're right—L.C.'s grandmother comes home today."

"When will we know…you know… about everything? She'll tell us if she found something, right?" asked Troy.

"We can talk to her tomorrow," said Becky as she tried to gather her hair into a ponytail. "L.C. said she'd be working at the **maritime** museum in Southport, and she promised to tell us if she found anything. Somehow I think L.C. is pretty good at keeping her promises."

**maritime** ❋
(MARE-i-time)
Anything having to do with the sea, for example, maritime law.

"You know," said Troy slowly, "none of us said it, but do we all think the guy talking to us was Blackbeard?"

"You mean do we all think that guy was Blackbeard's ghost?" corrected Sam.

"Okay, okay," said Troy. "Blackbeard's ghost."

"Who—I mean—what else could it be?" asked Andrew. "Who else—I mean—what else would still have a totally black beard when the rest of his hair was all gray? What I want to know is why he was so interested in that little lighthouse at Price's Creek."

**✳ruins**

(ROO-inz)
The stones, bricks, wood, and other building materials that remain after a structure has collapsed.

"Exactly," said Becky. "It's just a stack of bricks. You can't climb to the top or even go see the **ruins**. Why would that old guy say that the Price's Creek Lighthouse was helpful?"

"And what was up with that poem?" Sam wrinkled his nose as he remembered the rhyme recited by the bearded man.

"I don't know," said Troy. "It was pretty bad, but I did write it down in my journal:"

Watch the flash, mind the light,
Heed the warning beam so bright.
Through darkest night and stormy seas
They light the way and bring ye peace.

Andrew spoke up. "And wasn't it a little weird that he recited the poem right when we could see all three lighthouses—the Oak Island Lighthouse, Old Baldy over on Bald Head Island, and the little Price's Creek Lighthouse?"

Behind them, someone cleared his throat and said, "Ahh, technically speaking, the Price's Creek light is not a lighthouse."

# Chapter 3
# Ferry Tales

Troy, Andrew, Sam, and Becky were so busy talking about Blackbeard (or rather Blackbeard's ghost) that they hadn't noticed the uniformed man standing at the rail beside them. He was dressed in **khaki** pants, a khaki shirt, and a North Carolina Ferry System baseball cap. His name tag said "J. Hernandez."

**khaki**
(KHAA-key)
A light brown or tan color.

"First time on a ferry, son?" Mr. Hernandez nodded at Sam who was still gripping the side of the boat.

Sam looked a little embarrassed. "No, sir. I've been on a ferry before, just not on one where the cars and trucks go along too. Our ferries just take people back and forth across the bay."

"You're not from around here, are you?" asked Mr. Hernandez.

"I'm not, but these guys are. My sister and I are from California—near San Francisco—and we're on our way to the Fort Fisher Aquarium. The last time I was on a ferry, the waves were choppy and I almost fell in."

"Well then, you'll like our ferry. This is a calmer crossing because we cross a river instead of an open bay like you have in San Francisco. Also, the weight of all the vehicles on board makes the ride steadier."

"Look, Sam! I don't need to hold on at all," said Troy.

He held up both hands and turned completely around—**360 degrees**—to show that he could keep his balance even while turning in a circle.

**360 degrees** 🞧

(360 de-GREEZ)
The measurement of a full circle. (90 degrees is 1/4 of a circle; 180 degrees is 1/2 of a circle; 270 degrees is 3/4 of a circle.)

Mr. Hernandez shook his head at Troy. "I don't know that I'd go that far, son. It's always better to be safe than sorry. Not too long ago we had sort of a rogue wave that was a lot bigger than our normal waves. It slammed right into the ferry, and several folks got hurt. Some of the cars were pushed into each other and got all banged up."

Mr. Hernandez pointed at a huge ship off in the distance. "We think the wave might have came from one of those container ships moving too fast. Rogue waves are pretty rare, but I wouldn't take any chances— anything's possible."

"Excuse me, sir," said Andrew, "if it's not a lighthouse, what is it?"

"You mean the Price's Creek light? It's called a range light—actually it's one half of a pair of range lights," said Mr. Hernandez shading his eyes and looking at the falling-down tower of bricks back on the shore.

"Like lighthouses, range lights help captains steer their ships safely. But instead of a light that can be seen from far away—like the one in the Oak Island Lighthouse—range lights use a pair of shorter lights."

Mr. Hernandez used his hands to explain how the range lights work. He put both hands up side-by-side. It looked like he was giving Andrew a double high five. His left hand was out in front a bit and a little lower than his right hand.

"The two lights are built one behind the other—the back light is taller than the front one. When a captain first sees the range

lights through a spyglass, they look like
they're side by side. The captain heads the
ship toward the taller light.

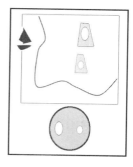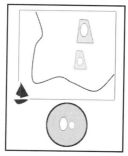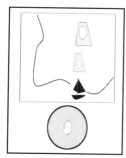

"As the ship travels up the river, the
two lights look like they are getting closer
together.

Mr. Hernandez motioned with his head.
"Go ahead, Andrew. You be the ship. Take
three giant steps to your right. Do my hands
look closer together?"

"They do!" said Andrew.

"Keep moving up the river," said Mr.
Hernandez. "Take three more steps to your
right and come around this way. Now tell me
what you see."

"They're lined up! I can only see both of your hands because your right hand is up higher."

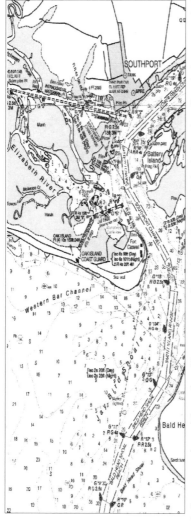

"Exactly," said Mr. Hernandez. "The captain knows that when the range lights line up, it's time to look up the river and find the next pair of lights. Then he does the same thing with the new set."

"How do the captains know where to find the range lights?" asked Andrew.

"Captains have a lot of maps—they call them charts—and these charts show all the navigational aids in the area, including

32

buoys, lighthouses, and range lights. The
Cape Fear River has lots of twists and turns,
so the range lights help boats and ships stay
in the middle of the river where the water
is deepest. As long as the captain keeps his
ship headed toward the taller light, he won't
run aground—unless, of course, the river has
changed because of a storm or high winds or
shifting sands or something like that."

"Do they still use range lights?" asked
Sam. "The Price's Creek light is almost all
torn down. It looks pretty old."

"You would look old too if you were built
back in 1849. The U.S. Government built
eight range lights to help ships navigate the
Cape Fear River to the Port of Wilmington."
Mr. Hernandez pointed up the river.

"And then the Civil War started. The
Confederate troops used the range lights to
help the ships that were smuggling supplies
to the Confederate Army. The Confederate
soldiers also used the range lights to

send signals between Fort Fisher—" Mr. Hernandez pointed across the river. "and Fort Caswell over there on Oak Island." He pointed toward the Oak Island Lighthouse.

"Eventually the Union Army captured Wilmington and took control of the Cape Fear River. But as the Confederate soldiers retreated, they tore down the range lights so the Union soldiers couldn't use them. All the lights were destroyed except the ones at Price's Creek."

"But there's only one range light there now, isn't there?" Sam looked confused.

"You're right. Only one survived. There used to be another lighthouse behind that little guy. It was taller and bigger because the lighthouse keeper and his family lived there. It was damaged in the Civil War and then a couple of hurricanes finished it off. Eventually it just fell down. Somebody told me that a guy used the bricks to build a house in Southport."

"Does Price's Creek Lighthouse—I mean range light—still have a light?" asked Troy.

"It's okay to call it a lighthouse, Troy. Nowadays, some range lights are just lights on a buoy, but the Price's Creek light really does have a house—even if it's falling down. But no, the light itself is long gone."

"Can we go see the building that's still there?" asked Becky.

"There's not much to see, I'm afraid," said Mr. Hernandez. "It's on private land, and the owner is being awfully slow about restoring it." He shook his head sadly. "Yep, it won't be too much longer before that little fellow just crumbles into the swamp. It's a shame too—it's the smallest lighthouse in North Carolina, but it sure has seen a lot of history."

Mr. Hernandez took off his cap and then settled it back on his head with a sigh. "For a while there we all thought the current owner would let one of the historical groups take it over and restore it. They did let some lighthouse folks go out to see the place, but nothing ever came of it.

"So now, the best place to see what's left of the Price's Creek Lighthouse is right here on the ferry. And the only ones who visit the light are Allie Alligator and her children— and maybe a few ghosts."

## Chapter 4
# Stede's Ending

"Ghosts?" said Troy innocently.

He exchanged quick glances with the others.

"Well, there should be some ghosts," said Mr. Hernandez. "Right over there is where ol' Stede Bonnet was finally captured. Have you ever heard of Stede Bonnet? He was a pirate who roamed these waters back before the American Revolutionary War."

"A pirate, you say," echoed Andrew slowly.

"Hmmm," said Becky carefully, "I wonder if Stede Bonnet had any treasure. Mr. Hernandez, did you ever hear anything about Stede Bonnet having any sort of treasure here?"

"Well, I never heard anything specific, but any pirate worth his salt would have treasure. I do know that Blackbeard himself took over Stede Bonnet's ship for a time, and they did not part on good terms. I always heard that Blackbeard chased Stede Bonnet all over the place, and I just assumed it was because he wanted Bonnet's treasure."

Sam looked quickly at Troy, Becky, and Andrew, but he couldn't stand it any longer. He just had to ask.

"Mr. Hernandez, if Stede Bonnet did have a treasure, don't you think he would have left some clues? And don't you think he would have buried it around here? And don't you think…" Sam stopped and clamped his hand over his own mouth.

Becky just shook her head slowly.

"It *would* make sense that Stede Bonnet's treasure was hidden somewhere around here," agreed Mr. Hernandez. "If it was me, I would hide my treasure somewhere close by and then try to lead Blackbeard in the other direction."

A sudden blast of the ferry's loud horn made Sam, Becky, Troy, and Andrew jump and Mr. Hernandez grin.

"We're about to dock and I'm needed up front at the bow lines," he said. "It was a pleasure to meet you all. Let me know if you have any more questions." He shook hands all around.

"Enjoy your visit to the aquarium. Maybe we'll see you when you come back across the river. And, Sam?"

"Yes, sir?"

"Keep hanging on, and watch out for those seagulls. They can be messy."

Mr. Hernandez touched the brim of his cap in a salute, and then hurried off to help with the docking of the boat.

"What did he mean by that?" Sam wondered out loud.

"Well," said Troy, looking up carefully at the sky, "if the seagulls are flying right over you, they sometimes...you know. Like that!"

Troy wrinkled his nose and pointed as something fell on the deck right in front of Sam.

## Chapter 5
# Hunting Scavengers

After the ferry docked, it was only a few minutes before Sam, Becky, Troy, Andrew, and the rest of the group walked into the North Carolina Aquarium at Fort Fisher.

"Scavenger hunt? Anyone want to do the scavenger hunt?"

Aquarium employees were handing out papers that looked like treasure maps. Anyone who wanted to join in the fun of searching for the items on the list could take a paper.

A smiling young woman came up to Troy. She was dressed in an old-fashioned costume rather than in the modern uniforms of the other aquarium workers. In her hand was a piece of paper that looked like an old **parchment**.

✳**parchment**
(PARCH-munt)
Parchment is made from animal skin stretched, scraped, and dried so it can be written on. Most people today use paper that looks like parchment, but is made from plants.

"Is this your first time here?" she asked.

"My brother and I visited here once before, but our friends have never been here."

"You're Lila's friends aren't you?"

"Yes, but how…" started Becky.

But the girl continued. "Then this is for you." She handed Troy the paper. "You'll want to start with the whale exhibit downstairs. Have a great visit!"

A crowd came in right behind them, so, with a wave at their parents and Eden,

Troy, Andrew, Sam, and Becky followed the signs to the lower level. Along the way, they passed all sorts of fascinating sights. There were exhibits about the local fish— both freshwater and saltwater—and exhibits about snakes, turtles, and even crocodiles.

The aquarium's most famous resident, Luna the **albino** alligator, had moved in with her crocodile cousins. She was quietly watching the people rushing by as if she was waiting for someone. With her white skin, she looked like a ghost alligator.

albino ✳
(al-BY-no)
A person or animal with no color pigment because of a genetic condition. This lack of color usually shows up as white hair, white skin, and red eyes. For example, instead of having the usual olive green, brown, gray, or black skin of other alligators, Luna is all white.

"We've got to hurry," said Troy leading the way. "That whale program will start without us."

"Wait!" Andrew stopped suddenly and pointed. "Is that diver talking underwater?"

43

Sam was trying to catch a glimpse of what seemed to be a really huge shark, and he didn't stop.

"Ooof! Sorry, Andrew!"

Two seconds later, Becky, walking backward and watching a seagull that had snuck into the aquarium without buying a ticket, bumped into Sam, who bumped into Andrew...again.

"Ooof! Sorry, Sam! Sorry, Andrew!" said Becky.

✳**auditorium**
(aw-di-TORE-e-um)
A room where many people can see a play or easily listen to a speaker, choir, orchestra, or similar event.

"Here it is!" said Troy. *He* had been paying attention and didn't bump into anyone.

"It's called 'Where's Waldo Whale?' and it's here in the **auditorium**. Come on!"

"But Troy! That underwater guy is answering questions from the audience!"

Andrew wasn't sure he wanted to leave. The diver was hanging out with eels, rays, and sharks in—according to the sign—a 235,000-gallon tank that re-created the habitat of the infamous Frying Pan shoals.

"We can come back, Andrew," said Troy, pulling on his brother's arm. "The whale program is starting *now*!"

## Chapter 6
# Shadow Watching

"Where have you all been?"

Dad and Mr. Jamison caught up with Troy, Becky, Sam, and Andrew at the moray eel cave.

"Did you see Luna?" Dad asked with a huge smile on his face. "Did you see the diver that talked underwater? Did you see the **Megalodon**? Did you pat the horseshoe crab? This place is awesome!"

**Megalodon** ✳
(MEG-a-la-don)
An extinct species of monster shark that—according to some fossil findings—was 60 feet long and ate whales.

Becky replied, "Yes. Yes. I don't think so, and ouch! Did you really pat a horseshoe crab? Did it pinch you?"

"We didn't pat its claws," said Mr. Jamison coming up behind Dad, "just its shell. And I have to say, I think he liked it."

"He liked it when *I* was patting him," said Dad, "but he looked a little uncomfortable when you were doing it. You were patting him too hard."

"How do you know he looked unhappy? Could you see his eyes?"

"No, but he held his shell differently. He was definitely happier when *I* was patting him."

"You can't tell that just from touching his shell."

"Can too. I'm very sensitive."

Sam and Troy looked at their dads and then at each other. Troy shook his head, but Sam just grinned.

"Let's go," said Andrew. "They're going to do this forever."

"Did we find everything on the scavenger hunt list and answer all the questions?" asked Sam.

"Almost," said Andrew. "Most of it had to do with the whale program. The last question is 'What is your favorite exhibit in the aquarium?' We can do that one later."

"You're right," said Becky. "Let's go find that new bald eagle. I bet that's where Mom is. She loves eagles."

"Do they have an octopus?" asked Troy. "I've always wanted to see one up close."

49

"I bet they do—maybe in that tank with the flounder. Did you see that thing? Both his eyes are on top—like he's lying on his stomach. It's pretty weird." Sam rolled his eyes around and around trying to look like a flounder.

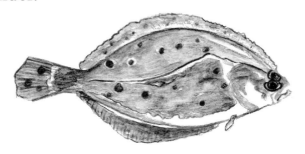

Becky laughed and followed Sam up the stairs. "You'd make a terrible flounder, Sam."

Andrew trailed the others. He was reading something about seahorses, so he walked slowly. If he hadn't dropped the scavenger hunt paper and turned around to pick it up, he might never have noticed the man with gray-almost-white hair and a bushy black beard standing in a corner by the shark tank.

But the man wasn't looking at the sharks—he was looking right at Andrew.

Andrew hurried to catch up to the others. He grabbed Becky's arm and whispered. "Becky, look!"

But when they turned to look, the man was gone.

"What is it, Andrew?" asked Becky.

"Nothing...I guess. At least it's nothing now."

"What was it before?"

"A guy with white hair and a really black beard...watching us."

## Chapter 7
# A Whale of a Tale

Becky, Sam, Troy, and Andrew waited outside the aquarium for their parents. They sat beside the flying fish fountain sculpture and watched the starlings splashing in their own personal birdbath. It was past closing time, but Mom and Dad were still having a conversation with the aquarium **docents**.

**docents** ✳
(DOE-sent)
Experts who answer questions and help people enjoy their visit at, for example, a museum, aquarium, or art gallery.

"Are Mom and Dad still talking?" Sam looked up from the ferry schedule he was reading. "Unless we leave right now, we're going to miss the last ferry back to Southport."

Ten minutes later, chatting and laughing, Mom, Dad, and Mrs. Jamison walked out of the aquarium. Mr. Jamison followed, carrying a sleeping Eden on his shoulder. They stopped at the flying fish fountain.

"Those are the nicest people," sighed Mom. "I could have talked with them all night long. They answered every single 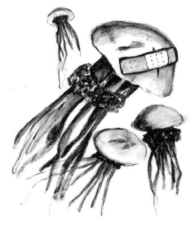 one of my questions. Mike was just starting on his questions, but they said there was some sort of jellyfish emergency and they needed all the docents to help."

"We offered to help," said Dad, "but they said something about these being North Carolina jellyfish and us being from California so there would be lots of forms to fill out… Anyway, they seemed to think they had it under control."

"You *know* we missed the ferry back to Southport, don't you?" said Sam.

He let the question hang in the air so the parents could see the consequences of their less-than-responsible actions.

"We're not going back on the ferry," said Dad.

"We *know* that," muttered Sam.

"How are we getting home?" asked Troy.

"We're going a different way," said Dad cheerfully.

"We know that too," said Becky.

"A way we haven't been yet," added Mr. Jamison.

"We also pretty much figured that out," said Andrew. "Want to tell us how we're getting back?"

"Nope. Hey, how did you kids do on the scavenger hunt?" asked Mr. Jamison, changing the subject as everyone piled into the van. "*We* found everything on the list."

"Wasn't that scavenger hunt just for kids?" Troy asked, raising his eyebrows.

"Not necessarily," said Dad. "I'm sure lots of adults did it too." He grinned at Mr. Jamison. "But I bet they didn't do as well as we did! High five, Ed!"

Dad and Mr. Jamison did a very awkward high five and then tried for a follow-up fist bump.

Troy raised his eyebrows even higher, while Sam groaned and hid his face in his hands. Becky and Andrew just stared, shaking their heads slowly.

"Aw, c'mon," said Mr. Jamison. "Some things on the list were really hard to find. Those tiny butterflies and the climate change indicators? Did you find all of those?"

"We must have had a different list," said Andrew. "We didn't have anything about climate change or butterflies."

"Except for finding Luna," added Troy, "all of our items were about the whale-tracking program, and how they use **latitude** and **longitude** to locate whales anywhere on Earth."

latitude and longitude
(LAT-i-tood and LAWN-ji-tood) Imaginary lines on a globe or map used to identify specific locations on Earth.

"Latitude?" asked Dad.

"And longitude," said Becky.

"I always used to get those mixed up," confessed Mr. Jamison. "Then my friend told me to remember 'fat lat' and think about the earth having a big belly with latitude lines that go around it like a belt."

"That's good," agreed Dad. "Fat lat. So, if latitude lines are the horizontal ones,

that leaves longitude lines to be the long, vertical ones that go between the North and South Poles."

"What else did you find out about latitude and longitude?" asked Mom as she steered the van out of the parking lot.

"We learned how you write the latitude and longitude for a place," said Sam. "It's a lot like writing a time because it has minutes and seconds. But it's not quite the same because instead of hours you use degrees."

"Degrees?" asked Dad, wrinkling his forehead. "You mean like degrees on a thermometer?"

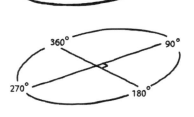

"Nooo, Dad," said Becky patiently, "degrees like the measurements on a circle. You know, a right angle is 90 degrees. Or, like when we were up on top of the Oak

Island Lighthouse and we could see in every direction—that's a 360-degree view."

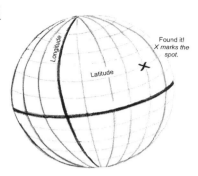

Found it!
X marks the spot.

"So," Sam said, "no matter where something is on Earth, if you know its latitude and longitude, you can probably find it."

"Wildlife people track the movements of all sorts of animals with latitude and longitude," added Becky. "These guys were tracking dolphins and whales."

**blubber**
(BLUB-burr)
The layer of fat between a whale's skin and muscles.

"It's really cool," said Troy. "They put a little tag transmitter thing right in the **blubber** under the whale's skin."

"And then," said Becky, "whenever the whale comes up for air, that tag transmits the date and time along with the latitude and longitude of its location."

Troy took over again. "Satellites pick up the transmission, and then people tracking the whales can download the information and see where the whales have been."

"Do they put tags on all the whales?" asked Dad.

"No," said Troy, "just a few. The whales travel around in groups—"

"Pods," said Andrew, still looking at the scavenger hunt papers he had in his hands. "The whale groups are called pods…"

He raised his head and saw everybody looking at him. "Sorry, Troy," he muttered.

Troy started again. "The whales travel around in *pods*, so you don't need to tag all of them. Besides, it costs a ton of money— the aquarium guy said it could be up to five thousand dollars just to buy one tag for one whale. Then you still have to pay somebody to put the tag in the whale's blubber."

"My gracious," said Mom. "I had no idea it was so expensive. No wonder they ask people to donate money to help."

"They told us that the whale population is growing again because of these tracking things," Sam said. "If the whales get in trouble—like if they get tangled up in a fishing net or hurt by a ship's propeller—people can help them because they know where the whales are."

"The whale tracking exhibit and the latitude and longitude stuff took most of our time," said Becky. "Andrew is just now finishing our crossword puzzle."

"A crossword puzzle!" said Mrs. Jamison. "We didn't get a crossword puzzle did we, Alice? I *love* crossword puzzles." She folded her arms across her chest and stuck out her bottom lip like a little kid.

Becky burst out laughing. "It was just a *little* crossword puzzle, Mrs. Jamison. It didn't even seem to have that much to do with the aquarium—did it, Andrew? Andrew?"

Becky looked over at Andrew who was still studying the scavenger hunt papers. On his face was a very big frown.

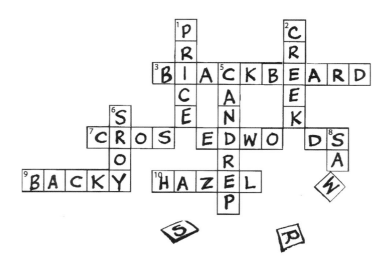

# Chapter 8
# Crossed Words

While the chatter continued in the front seats, Becky leaned over to Andrew. "Why are you still looking at that crossword puzzle? It's all finished, isn't it?"

In a very quiet voice, Andrew said, "I'm wondering why *our* scavenger hunt is the only one on this kind of paper. And I'm wondering why we're the only ones who got a crossword puzzle."

"I don't understand," said Becky. "What do you mean?"

"The people in front of us at the aquarium left their scavenger hunt on the bench," said Andrew. "I pulled this one out of the recycling bin, and this is the one our parents had. All of these are the same. Everyone did the same scavenger hunt—except us."

"Why would we get a whole different scavenger hunt and puzzle?" asked Becky.

I don't know, but check out these clues for our crossword puzzle: 'The costs of things'?"

"Price?"

"Costs. Plural. And it's six letters."

"Okay, prices."

"How about 'a small river'? Five letters."

"Stream? No that's six letters. Creek?"

"Okay, what's a 'tall navigational aid for ships'?"

"Lighthouse?"

"Put them together and you have…"

"Price's Creek Lighthouse," said Becky softly in surprise. "What else does it say?"

"Listen to this clue," said Andrew reading from the paper. "'Dishonorable, traitorous, black-hearted, black-bearded, back-stabbing, scallywag pirate who chased the noble Stede Bonnet to his death and tried to steal Bonnet's greatest treasure but FAILED!'"

Becky sat back in her seat. "That's a pretty weird clue. By any chance, does 'Blackbeard' fit in the space?"

"Yeah…it fits perfectly, and the last clue is 'Watch out for.' It has six letters."

"'Beware' would fit," said Troy. He and Sam had been listening.

"Exactly," said Andrew. "And we're the only ones who have this puzzle."

"But that girl was giving them out to everybody, wasn't she?" asked Sam.

Becky thought for a moment. "Were there any other aquarium people in costumes?"

"They were wearing the same kind of shirt and pants," offered Troy.

"So the only person wearing an old-fashioned costume was the girl who gave us this paper," said Troy slowly. "And now we think our scavenger hunt is different from all the others?"

"Did you tell Troy and Sam what you thought you saw in the aquarium?" Becky said to Andrew.

"He told us," said Sam, "but why would Blackbeard's ghost be following us to the aquarium? It's a great place, but there's no pirate treasure there."

"Maybe he thought we were getting another piece of the puzzle that would help us find the treasure," said Troy.

"Were we?" asked Becky.

"Not that I know of," said Sam.

Troy shook his head.

"Did you guys see the finished puzzle?" asked Andrew. He handed Troy the paper with all the answers to the crossword puzzle filled in. Troy held the puzzle so Sam and Becky could see too.

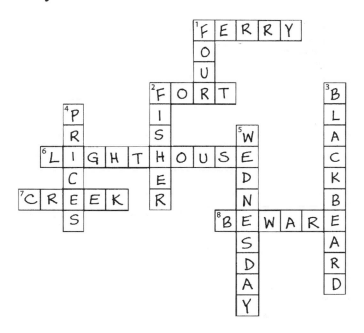

"It's just a crossword puzzle with weird clues," said Becky. "Isn't it?"

"Read all the answers when I put them together like this," said Andrew.

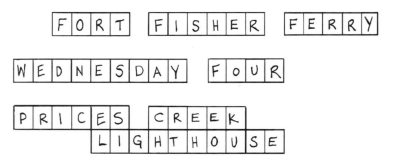

"Somebody is trying to send us a message," whispered Sam.

"You're right," said Troy. "

"Yeah," said Becky, "and the rest of the message says 'Beware Blackbeard'."

## Chapter 9
# Hills, Thrills, and Chills

"We're almost here," called Dad from the front seat.

"Where is 'here,' Dad?" Becky looked out the window to see if she could figure it out.

The short drive had kept ocean views on their right and a nonstop parade of sea oats and **pastel** beach houses on their left.

"Carolina Beach!" sighed Mr. Jamison. "I see Ferris wheels, skeeball, and doughnuts in our future!"

**pastel**
(pass-TELL)
Colors that have a lot of white to make them seem soft and delicate.

Dad looked sad. "No ice cream?"

"Just wait, Mike," replied Mr. Jamison in a soothing voice. "If cold milk and these special doughnuts don't do the trick, I will personally buy you the biggest ice cream cone you can eat."

"AND cotton candy?" asked Dad.

"Mike!" Mom looked **stern**.

"Okay, okay. But just for the record, I can eat a *lot* of ice cream."

"We'll see," said Mr. Jamison.

"No way am I missing out on this," said Sam as he jumped out from the back seat.

"Me either," said Becky. "I've known Dad all my life and I've never known him to eat anything other than—oh, look! It's a double Ferris wheel! Can we go on it, Mom? I bet we can see all the way to Oak Island from up there!"

*stern
(stirn)
Very serious, even disappointed. Sometimes angry.*

70

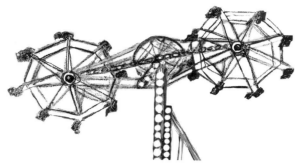

"Weeell...okay," said Mom. "I do think we should do rides first—before we eat our weight in doughnuts."

"Good idea," said Andrew, looking at Troy. "Sometimes Ferris wheels make my stomach jumpy."

Troy frowned and nodded in agreement.

The line was short, and before long, Mom and Becky, Andrew and Mrs. Jamison, and Sam and Troy were rising in the air to get a bird's-eye view of Carolina Beach, the Cape Fear River, and the Atlantic Ocean.

"Look," said Becky, pointing. "Is that the light from the Oak Island Lighthouse? Can we see it from here?"

"I can't tell," called Andrew from his seat beside his mom. "I don't think so—it's too low. Maybe it's the lighthouse on Bald Head Island."

"It can't be the light at Bald Head," said Mrs. Jamison. "That light is very dim—you can barely see it across the river at Oak Island."

"I feel sorry for that little Price's Creek range light," Sam said to Troy. "If it had a light, it would be right…over…there, by those smokestacks, right?"

"You mean right there, where that light is?" asked Troy, squinting his eyes and pointing.

But by this time, he and Sam were on their way back down the other side of the Ferris wheel. With a *whoosh!* they swept by the loading platform and then swooped up into the air again. This time there was no doubt about it.

From a dark swamp on the shore of the Cape Fear River was a small but determined light shining across the water.

"Look, Sam!" said Troy. "What *is* that?"

"'Watch the flash, mind the light...' That's what the poem said, right?" said Sam. He looked at Troy. "We saw the flash at the Oak Island Lighthouse. Do you think this is the light we're supposed to 'mind'?"

**descent** ✳
(dee-CENT)
Going down, as on an elevator or steps.

"What I think is that we definitely need to be on that Fort Fisher ferry at four o'clock tomorrow," said Troy.

He kept his eyes on the light shining across the river until the Ferris wheel whisked them down for their final **descent**.

# Chapter 10
# Rerouting

It turns out that Mr. Jamison was right: at least for tonight, Dad was officially a doughnut fan.

After a cup of milk and two doughnuts each—except for Eden, who was still working on her first one, and Dad who wanted "just one more"—everyone was back in the van, buckling seat belts.

"So, Dad," said Becky as she licked the last bit of doughnut glaze from her fingers, "if the ferry isn't running any more tonight, how are we getting back to our beach house?"

"Ed?" said Dad to Mr. Jamison.

"Boys?" said Mr. Jamison to Andrew and Troy.

"To the battleship!" chorused Troy and Andrew.

"We're taking a battleship home?" Sam wasn't sure he believed that, but it sounded exciting.

"No, silly," said Troy. "A battleship isn't a taxi."

Sam shrugged his shoulders. "I didn't know. I thought maybe 'battleship' was your code name for another kind of ferry or something. So, how is a battleship going to help us get home?"

"The road we take to get back goes to Wilmington and right by the USS *North Carolina*," explained Andrew.

"Wait a minute," said Becky. "Isn't Wilmington *north* of here? And isn't our house on Oak Island *south* of here? Why would we go north when we want to go south?"

"Short answer?" said Mr. Jamison, "Because the ferry stopped running for the night."

"It will take us about twice as long," added Dad, "but it's the only way to drive from Carolina Beach to Oak Island at this time of night."

"The good news," said Troy, "is that you get a great view of the battleship right from the road. It's pretty cool to see it parked—"

"Berthed," interrupted Andrew. "It's not parked, it's *berthed*. You don't park a battleship."

"*I* don't park *or* berth it," said Troy, annoyed at Andrew's interruption, "but the people who do, have berthed it across the river from downtown Wilmington. You can see it from all around."

"And you can tour the ship and see what happened to it during World War II," said Andrew. "It was in the Pacific and it helped protect the USS *Enterprise*, a huge aircraft carrier."

"The USS *North Carolina* is 700 feet long and weighs 36,000 tons," said Troy proudly. "That's, like, 72 million pounds! They said it had been sunk, six different times, but it never was. It's a good ship."

"So, aren't we actually going in kind of a loop?" asked Mom from the front seat. "We drive to Wilmington, cross the Cape Fear River on the drawbridge—we *can* go over the drawbridge, can't we, Ed?"

"As long as it's not drawn to let a boat go under it," chuckled Mr. Jamison.

Mom rolled her eyes and started again. "We drive to Wilmington, cross the river on the drawbridge—when it's not drawn—then we head back toward Oak Island on the other side. We cross one more bridge—you know, the one where you can see the Oak Island Lighthouse—and then we're home."

"I guess you could say we'll cross *that* bridge when we come to it," said Dad cheerily.

Even Mr. Jamison groaned.

But when the time came to cross that bridge, the only person who saw it, was Mom.

The Oak Island Lighthouse was keeping watch, but when Mom put down her window to sniff the fresh salt air and listen to the night noises, the only sounds she heard were gentle snores coming from inside the van.

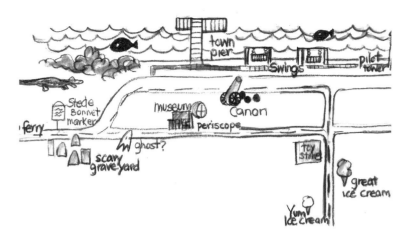

## Chapter 11
# Museum@Southport

In Southport the next morning, Mr. Jamison found a parking place by the river. "See you at the swings at one o'clock," he said to Mom, Mrs. Jamison, and Eden.

The moms had promised Eden a trip to the store that sold Christmas things all year long. Everyone else was walking to the maritime museum where L.C. worked. They were all meeting back at the big porch swings along the riverfront in a couple of hours to decide what to do for lunch and the afternoon.

Sam, Troy, Becky, and Andrew didn't really care what they did after their museum visit—as long as they were on the Fort Fisher Ferry at four o'clock that afternoon.

"Dad, we can go on the ferry without driving the van on, right?" Andrew was 99.9999 percent sure they could, but he didn't want to take any chances.

"Yep," answered Mr. Jamison. "You get your ticket and then just walk on after they load up all the cars. You do have to wait upstairs in the lounge area until the boat gets underway and again when they dock. Other than that, you can walk around just like you can when you drive on."

"Do you guys want to go on the ferry again?" asked Dad. "I'm all for that! We can leave the van, ride across, come right back, and still have plenty of time to get home to make the ice cream."

"Wow! L.C. gets to work here?"

Andrew stopped at the door to Southport's Maritime Museum, blocking traffic for everyone behind him.

"Go on in, Andrew," complained Troy. "You can't just stop in the doorway. The rest of us want to see too."

**artifacts** ✳

(ART-eh-faks)
Actual pieces of history that help scientists understand the past. For example, the Southport Maritime Museum has artifacts from 2,000-year-old canoes.

The Southport Maritime Museum has **artifacts** like buttons and porcelain plates from the 1725 settlement of Brunswick Town. It has shrimp nets, model ships, and a Megaladon shark tooth. You can learn about Stede Bonnet's final days as a pirate, and you can even look through a periscope

that was once on the deep-diving, research submarine, the USS *Dolphin*.

Becky was the first to spot L.C., who was helping a customer in the museum gift shop. Becky waved and then waited for L.C. to finish talking with the visitor.

"Thank you, ma'am," said L.C., smiling at her guest. "I hope your grandson enjoys that book. The author is one of our best sellers for kids' books. Enjoy your time in Southport!"

L.C. waved and smiled at Becky. "I've been waiting for you guys! Give me a minute while I see if I can take my lunch now."

She leaned over the counter toward Becky and whispered, "I have something to show you all!"

# Chapter 12
# An Ill Wind

L.C. led the way outside to the porch in front of the museum. It was deserted except for four rocking chairs and one small table. L.C. carried her lunch and a cloth bag. She was grinning from ear to ear.

"Did your grandmother have the key?" asked Becky before anyone could even sit down.

"Did you get the trunk open?" asked Andrew.

"Was there anything inside?" asked Sam.

Troy's question was the loudest. "Did you find Stede Bonnet's greatest treasure?"

L.C. laughed and set the cloth bag on the table. "Yes, yes, yes, and I don't know," she replied. "Grandmother did have the key. We opened the trunk, and this is what was inside. What do you think?"

※**somber**

(SOM-burr)
Very serious and no-nonsense. Sometimes angry or unhappy.

L.C. carefully pulled three items from the bag. The first was a very old picture sketched in pencil. It showed three children: one girl and two boys. Each child held a book, and behind the children rose a stack of more books under three palm trees. The children in the picture looked very **somber**.

The second item that L.C. pulled out of the bag was a rolled-up piece of parchment. The third item was a heavy locket on a chain.

"So," repeated L.C., "what do you think?"

Her question hung in the air until Sam broke the silence.

"That's all?"

L.C. nodded. "Do you think the locket is Stede Bonnet's greatest treasure?" she asked.

Troy wrinkled his nose. "Not for a pirate!"

"I agree," nodded L.C. "I guess it could be this—it has a poem written on it."

She handed the rolled-up parchment to Becky. "It isn't very good. If I'd written it, I definitely wouldn't call it my greatest treasure."

"Read it," said Sam and Troy together.

Becky carefully unrolled the stiff parchment and read the poem:

Watch the flash, mind the light,
See the welcome beam so bright.
For windy storms can hide the day,
and Blackness oft obscures the way.
But friends know where the treasure be;
The twin holds all and kin the key.

Becky looked puzzled as she rolled up the parchment. She handed it back to L.C. who carefully tucked it into the bag.

"It starts out like the other poem, doesn't it?" said Sam. "But who is Ken?"

"K-I-N, not K-E-N," corrected Becky. "It means relatives or someone related to you."

"How did Stede Bonnet know we were twins?" blurted out Troy. "And I'm not holding *anything*—are you, Andrew?"

Andrew shook his head.

"I asked Grandmother if she recognized the children in the picture," said L.C. "She didn't, but she said it was the kind of picture that people paid artists to draw of their families a long time ago.
The girl in the picture is wearing a locket that looks like this one."

L.C. held up the locket for everyone to see. The letter B was **engraved** on the front.

"I got to the museum early today so I could look something up. Stede Bonnet had four children: one daughter named Mary, and three sons. The first boy died when he was just a baby."

**engraved**
(in-GRAVED)
Writing or drawings carved into metal or paper.

"That's sad," said Becky. "I can see why Stede Bonnet would call his children his greatest treasure—especially if one of them had died."

"Have we seen this picture before?" Sam scrunched his eyes. "That girl looks familiar." He wrinkled his forehead trying to remember where he'd seen the girl in the picture.

A loud *crash!* in the museum grabbed everyone's attention.

"What was that?" said L.C. as she turned toward the noise.

There was another, louder *crash!* and everyone rushed toward the museum entrance.

"It sounds like it's coming from the pirate exhibit," said L.C.

She was right. When they reached the exhibit, the picture of Stede Bonnet was lying on the floor with broken glass all around it. Pictures of other pirates had also fallen. In fact, the only picture left on the wall was a picture of Blackbeard.

"That's weird," muttered Becky.

"Too weird," agreed Troy.

"I'd better get someone to help me fix this," said L.C. She walked to the gift shop and picked up the phone. As she waited for someone to answer, she looked out the window. Outside on the porch, her lunch sat on the table along with the bag containing the items from Stede Bonnet's trunk. But something was wrong.

"Hey, guys," she called. "Did somebody take that poem out of my bag?"

"Nope," said Becky as she walked to the counter.

"Not me," said Sam, right behind Becky.

"Wasn't me," said Andrew. "Are you sure you put it away?"

"Don't you remember? Becky rolled it up and I put it back in the bag."

"I didn't take it out," called Troy from the entrance. He was on his way back out to the porch, but just as he put his hand on the doorknob, the wind—or something—flung open the door and then slammed it shut.

Troy jumped back in surprise. "Wow," he said. "What was that?"

"Maybe it was the wind?" suggested Andrew.

"Maybe…" said Becky with a shiver. "Maybe a wind called Blackbeard that takes poems out of bags and throws pictures on the floor."

"Blackbeard? If that was him, do you think he saw the crossword puzzles we left out there?" said Troy.

L.C. looked confused, so Troy explained how they

were the only ones to receive a scavenger hunt with a crossword puzzle, and how the answers to the crossword puzzle sounded like a meeting time and place.

"We're not sure what it means," admitted Troy, "but we're planning to be on the Fort Fisher Ferry at four o'clock this afternoon."

"Wait, that's it!" said Sam. "That's who the girl in the picture reminds me of!"

He took a deep breath and said slowly, "The girl who gave us the scavenger hunt at the aquarium is the same girl in the sketch that L.C. found in the trunk!"

"If that's true," said Becky, "then we got our scavenger hunt from Stede Bonnet's daughter, Mary."

"You're right!" whispered Andrew.

Troy nodded, his eyes wide.

"Okay," said L.C. slowly, "so you guys are going to be on the ferry at four o'clock.

What if there's a long line and you can't drive on?"

"We've already thought of that," said Troy. "We're going to walk on the ferry, get off on the other side and then get right back on so we can ride the same ferry back."

Sam chuckled. "My dad is making ice cream for dessert tonight. You can imagine how excited he is about that, and how much he would hate it if we missed the ferry and dinner was late."

L.C. laughed. "I certainly hope the ferry is on time. Your dad missing a chance for ice cream would be a sad sight."

"Did someone say something about ice cream?"

Dad's ears were obviously tuned to any mention of ice cream, anytime, anywhere. He and Mr. Jamison had been on the other side of the museum, listening to old radio broadcasts about Hurricane Hazel.

"Did you know," said Dad, "that when Hurricane Hazel struck the Carolinas back on October 15, 1954, she made land right at the border between North Carolina and South Carolina? It was one of the worst storms ever to hit the area."

"Hey L.C.!" said Mr. Jamison. "How are you? Do you and your grandmother want to join us for ice cream tonight?"

"It sounds great, Mr. Jamison, but I'm afraid we can't tonight. It's Bingo Night at the community center and my grandmother never misses it. I help call out the numbers. Maybe I could come over tomorrow night— do you think there will be any ice cream left?"

**skeptical** ✳
(SKEP-ti-cull)
Unbelieving, doubtful.

L.C. looked hopeful for an instant, but then she saw all the **skeptical** faces. "I guess not," she said with a sigh.

Then she smiled. "Maybe next time."

"Excellent idea!" said Dad. "We'll plan another ice cream night just for L.C. I'll be in charge."

"Come on, kids," said Mr. Jamison. "We have to meet the ladies at the swings and figure out what we're doing for lunch. Take care, L.C. Please say 'hello' to your grandmother for me."

"I will, Mr. Jamison."

"See you soon, L.C.," said Becky. "We'll let you know how our ferry ride turns out."

L.C. winked. "I can't wait to hear *everything* about it!"

## Chapter 13
# All Aboard

When it's summer in North Carolina—
and especially at the beach—there's almost
always a chance of thunderstorms in the
afternoon. As the day heads toward evening,
air from the hot sand and warm water rushes
up to mix with cooler air creating huge,
puffy-white cumulous clouds. As the clouds
collect more of the warm, moist air, they get
darker and become thunderheads.

Today, thunderheads were looming on the
horizon, growing bigger and darker as the
day wore on.

"Those clouds are coming this way," said Mr. Jamison squinting at the sky. "We might get some rain."

"It's almost chilly when the sun goes behind one of those big ones," said Dad. "I think you're right about the rain, Ed. It's starting to get dark."

**✳pedestrians**
(peh-DESS-tree-uns)
People who are traveling on foot.

After all the vehicles that could fit were loaded onto the ferry, the bicyclers and the **pedestrians** walked across the loading ramp and headed up the stairs to the passengers' lounge. The captain blew the warning horn and the ferry started its 35-minute trip across the river.

Once the ferry was away from the dock, the captain blew the horn again. Sam, Becky, Troy, and Andrew scrambled down the steps and started toward the bow of the boat. The adults decided to stay on the upper deck to watch the approaching storm.

"Does anybody know why we're here on the ferry at four o'clock?" asked Andrew.

"Nope," said Becky, "but I do know that we're almost at the point where we can see all three lighthouses. Troy, you've got the **binoculars**. Look at the Bald Head Lighthouse. Do you see a light shining?"

**binoculars** *
(by-KNOCK-you-lars)
An instrument (like a microscope) that gives you a close-up look at things faraway. (Binoculars look like you put two pirate spy glasses side-by-side.)

"No. Or if there is, I can't see it from here."

All of a sudden, Sam shouted, "Guys—over here! Look at the Price's Creek Lighthouse!"

In front of them, on the other side of the river, from the square opening in an abandoned lighthouse that no one could visit, a light shone brightly out across the water.

"But…I thought Price's Creek didn't have a light!" whispered Becky.

"It doesn't—oh, wow!" said Andrew. "Quick, Troy! Can you see anyone there?"

"I don't see anybody," said Troy looking through the binoculars. "But I see the window where the light is coming from and… Wait, a minute, there's something in the window! It looks like words on a sign!"

"Can you read them?"

"No wait, it's not words—it's numbers. Somebody write this down! Thirty-three… fifty-two… Are you writing it down? Thirty-three, fifty-two, twenty-five…it looks like a minus seventy-eight…then two zeros… and ninety-four. Here, Andrew you look!"

Troy pulled the binoculars off over his head and handed them to his brother.

"You're right, Troy. I see the numbers. I can see—Oh, no! Everything's gone."

Troy took back the binoculars. "Yep, it's gone."

The light that seconds before had been shining out from the Price's Creek Lighthouse had vanished. In the shadowy light of the coming storm, you could barely see the lighthouse at all.

Troy looked over at his brother. "You saw the numbers, right?"

"I can't remember them all," said Andrew, "but I definitely saw numbers."

"And we all saw the light," said Sam.

"Did you get the numbers, Becky?" asked Troy.

They all looked at Becky, who had written down the numbers as Troy called them out.

"I did, but I don't know what they mean."

They all stared **mutely** at the little lighthouse for a minute or two.

**✳mutely**
(MEWT-lee)
With no talking or sound.

"We saw it," said Sam. "We all saw it, right?

"Right."

"And now it's gone."

"And," said Troy, "if we tell anyone what we saw, they'll laugh. Because it's an old, falling-down building that's almost a pile of bricks and there's no way light would be shining out of it."

"Light shining from where?" asked Dad walking up behind them. "I came to tell you all to come back up to the passenger lounge. The ferry is almost back at the Southport dock."

As they headed to the steps, Dad asked, "Did you guys see a light in the swamp over by the old Price's Creek Lighthouse? The crew was just telling us that they sometimes see **swamp gas** or reflections off the marsh at this time of day. They said it looks like lights coming from the lighthouse or somebody walking around with a flashlight. Of course, since it's private land, no one's allowed to be there at all. Is that the light you guys were talking about?"

**swamp gas** ❋

(swamp gas) Naturally occurring gas (mostly methane gas) that forms when swamp vegetation and other bio-degradable materials rot in an environment without oxygen. The stuff that's rotting—or decaying—makes a crust that keeps out the oxygen. As this vegetation breaks down, it gets hot and it produces methane gas. If the temperature gets hot enough, that gas can burst into flame.

"Ah....yeah, Dad," said Becky. "That's probably what we saw. Weird, isn't it?"

## Chapter 14
# Homemade Vanilla

If you ask, everyone will tell you their favorite flavor of homemade ice cream.

And then they will try to convince you that their favorite flavor should be your favorite flavor too.

When I was growing up, my grandfather Glen was the undisputed master of homemade ice cream. His favorite flavor was cherry vanilla with pecans, and I have to admit, it was deeeee-licious!

Now don't get me wrong. Cherry vanilla ice cream with pecans is good stuff, but for my money, peach is the only way to go.

Homemade peach ice cream, made the way my mama makes it, with fresh peaches, peach preserves, and almond flavoring—is without a doubt the best flavor in the world.

There is, however, a lot to be said for homemade vanilla ice cream.

Homemade vanilla ice cream (at least, my grandmother's recipe) needs nothing to make it perfect. But, if you *want* to, you can add just about anything. Fruit, cookies, chocolate syrup, caramel sauce, nuts, whipped cream—if you can name it, you can put it on vanilla ice cream. You can add strawberries that have been sliced with just a sprinkling of sugar to help them let go of their juices. Or, you can stir in chocolate chips. Yummm!

Making ice cream at the beach is a challenge. The weather is usually hot and humid, so the ice cream mixture has a hard time getting cold enough to freeze. You need a lot of ice in your ice-cream freezer, enough ice-cream salt, many arms to turn the crank, and tons of patience.

**consistency**
(Con-SIS-tents-see)
How thick, smooth, sticky, watery (and so on) something is.

Once the ice cream gets to a certain **consistency**, you might need help from your refrigerator's freezer to go from thick milkshake to ice cream. (Of course, if you're happy with milkshakes, just dig right in!)

\*\*\*\*\*

Dad supervised the making of the vanilla ice cream with a sharp eye. As Becky finished up her turning time, Dad took over the crank like a hand-off in a relay race.

As he cranked, he said, "Has everyone taken a turn? Hey, Sam did you get that? 'Taken a turn'?"

Troy burst out laughing, but Sam and Becky glared at him.

"Maybe you didn't know, Troy," said Sam slowly as if he were explaining something to a small child. "Mom, Becky, and I have a strict 'no laughing at puns' rule with Dad."

Becky nodded solemnly. "Dad thinks every pun he makes is the funniest thing ever, and he always laughs extremely loud at all of them. It's embarrassing, and we're trying to break him of the habit. So, we would appreciate it if you wouldn't encourage him by laughing."

"But he's funny," protested Troy. "I think he's funny. C'mon—you *know* he's funny."

Sam shook his head and stared sadly at Troy.

"Troy, my friend," said Dad, "if you ever find yourself in California, you come and stay with us. I like a man who enjoys a good pun."

"Everybody likes a *good* pun, Mike," said Mr. Jamison, who had taken over cranking the ice cream. "Do you know any?"

Now Becky was the one to burst out laughing. "Good one, Mr. Jamison!"

"Don't encourage him, Becky," said Andrew. "If you think your dad is bad about puns, you haven't heard ours."

**punt** ✳
(PUNT)
One meaning of punt (the one Dad uses here) means to give up, or try to do something a different way. You may have heard of a football team punting the ball, but did you know that punt is also a type of boat? (I didn't!)

"I think they're on to us, Ed," said Dad in a fake whisper. "It may be time for us to **punt**."

Everyone groaned.

Even Mr. Jamison held up his hands in defeat. "I'm done. I know when I'm beat. I bow to the master."

"You're not the only thing that's done, Ed," said Dad. "So's the ice cream!"

Dad took the crank off the top of the ice-cream freezer and pulled the cold metal cylinder full of soft, delicious ice cream from the bucket of slushy, salty, freezing-cold ice water.

He carefully wiped off the dripping container and headed toward the kitchen.

"Get those spoons ready!" he called over his shoulder.

## Chapter 15
# On the Beach

The next morning, after the breakfast dishes were washed and everything was cleaned up, Becky, Troy, and the moms drove to the grocery store while Sam, Andrew, Eden and the dads bought corn-on-the-cob from the produce stand and picked up that night's dinner from the fish market. By the time everyone returned home and put everything away, it was after three o'clock.

When Troy, Sam, Andrew, and Becky finally made their way down to the water, the beach was totally deserted.

In a couple of hours, the sun would sink closer to the western horizon and—family by family—people would come back out to enjoy the cooler air of the late afternoon and the beginning of a long summer evening.

But for right now, it was just too hot, and Sam, Becky, Andrew, and Troy were the only people on the beach.

Slathered with sunscreen and armed with hats and sunglasses, they walked slowly up the beach toward the Oak Island Lighthouse. They stayed on the hard sand, right at the edge of the water, because the soft sand was so hot that it burned the soles of their bare feet. Also, because walking on the hard sand meant they could wander off into the waves every once in a while to cool off their toes.

"Did you try subtracting?" asked Troy. He frowned as he studied the numbers Becky had written down during their ferry ride.

"Yes, 335,225 minus 780,094 is negative 444,869," said Becky. "Does that mean anything?"

"A phone number?" suggested Sam.

"Too short," said Becky.

"A zip code?"

"Too long," said Andrew. "Maybe the whole thing is a code. You know, one equals A, two equals B, and so on."

"What letter would you put for zero?" asked Sam. "And what do you do with the minus sign?"

"Hey, Troy," asked Becky, stopping to slap at a mosquito, "why did you say 'fifty-two' instead of 'five' and then 'two'? Why did you call out the numbers two at a time?"

"That's the way I saw them," answered Troy. "There was a little bit of space between them—like this."

With his finger, he wrote the numbers in the sand just as he'd seen them through the binoculars the night before.

"33, space, 52, space, 25, space, minus 78, space, 00, space, 94. That's what I saw."

Sam looked up from the paper and down at the numbers in the sand. He had a funny look on his face. "Hey, guys, what if the numbers were written like this:

33° 52' 25"

-78° 00' 94"

"Wait," said Becky, "that's how you write latitude and longitude."

"You're right!" said Troy. "It looks just like the numbers they used to locate the whales."

"I wonder what we'd find if we went to this location," said Andrew as they all stared at the numbers in the sand.

"Wait a minute!" said Becky. "Sam, you still have Mom's phone, don't you?"

"Yes…why?" Sam was **wary**.

"Get it out."

"Are you kidding?"
Sam squeaked, horrified at
Becky's suggestion.

**wary**
(WARE-ee)
Not trusting
someone or
something.

"Mom said it was 'just in case' and 'for emergencies only.' She also said that if I got it wet or if there was a single grain of sand on it, I'd have to pay for a new one. That's why it's in this bag."

Sam triumphantly pulled a zipped plastic bag out of his pocket. "And that's exactly where it's going to stay."

"Oh, I get it!" said Troy. "Does your mom have a **map app** on her phone, Becky?"

"Yep," said Becky, smiling.

"The one that gives you the latitude and longitude of places as well as the directions?" asked Andrew.

**map app**

(map app)
An application program for a computer or phone that can find a specific location on a map.

"Yep," said Becky, nodding and smiling even more.

"Sam," said Troy, "take the phone out of the bag. We need it."

"No way," said Sam.

"Sam," said Becky, "don't you get it? We can use these latitude and longitude numbers on the phone's map app."

"Why would we do that?" Sam held the zipped bag behind his back. "We have the latitude and longitude numbers right here."

"But, Sam," said Troy slowly, "instead of typing in a location to get the latitude and longitude numbers, what if we type in the latitude and longitude numbers to get the location?"

"Okay..." said Sam, and then his eyes got bigger. "Ohhhh!"

He pulled open the bag. "I'm pretty sure this counts as 'just in case.'"

"Be careful," warned Becky. "Remember, you have to pay for it if it gets wet!"

"Turn it on, Sam," said Andrew, "and find the map app."

"Type in the numbers," said Troy. "Do you want me to call them out to you"

"Hold on! My hands are wet and I don't have enough money to pay Mom."

"Here," said Becky, "use my towel. Do you want me to do it?"

"I can do it," said Sam. "Here, I've got it. Okay, Troy, read the numbers so I can make sure I've got them right."

Troy called out the numbers.

"Now search for it," said Becky.

"I *know*, Becky," said Sam. "Here goes."

Everyone held their breath as the small screen showed the phone making contact with a satellite 22,236 miles above them. It took just a few seconds for the phone to refocus back on Earth and show a bright red marker on a piece of land not too far from where they stood. The marker said:

Smith Island Museum of History
101 Lighthouse Wynd
Bald Head Island, NC
United States

Four sets of eyes looked at one another and then turned to look across the Cape Fear River to Bald Head Island.

## Chapter 16
# There Be Pirates

"Ahoy, kids!"

Dad and Mr. Jamison walked slowly up the beach toward Sam, Becky, Andrew, and Troy. Each dad held one of Eden's hands as she swung between them.

"Didn't you hear us calling?" asked Dad.

"Dinner's almost ready," said Mr. Jamison. "Your mothers sent us to get you."

"That's right," said Dad. "Everyone needs to get to bed early tonight so we can get an early start tomorrow. We have a lot to do."

"Tomorrow?" Troy wrinkled his forehead. "What's tomorrow, Dad?

"You're kidding, right? You don't know what tomorrow is?"

Mr. Jamison shook his head and then tossed Eden up in the air. "I don't know, Mike. Maybe we should just leave them at home."

Dad looked at Sam, Becky, Troy, and Andrew and sighed a very big sigh.

"I am disappointed," he said. "All this time I thought you were listening to every word I said. All the information I gave you... All the amazing stories...all the tips—oh, my gosh—all the jokes? You weren't listening to any of it."

Dad hung his head, shaking it slowly. He looked like he might cry.

"Gee, Dad," said Sam rolling his eyes. "Can you just tell us where we're going?

Because…" Sam glanced quickly back at the others. "Because there's somewhere we want to go too."

"Well, it will have to wait until next week," said Dad with a grin. (He seemed to be feeling much better.) "'Why will it have to wait?' you might ask. Well, I'll tell you why. Because we are going to Pirate Days! Ed and I already have our costumes."

**hoisting**
(HOYST-ing)
Raising a sail or flag, or picking up something to carry.

"That's right!" said Mr. Jamison, **hoisting** Eden to his shoulders. "And we've already agreed that we can both be captains so we can both wear cool hats. Arrrrgh!"

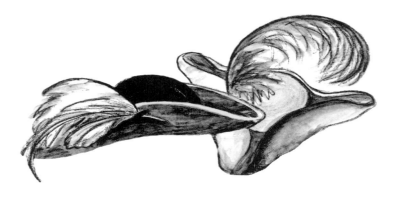

123

"Pirate Days?" repeated Andrew. "Isn't that over on…"

"Yep," said Dad. "we're spending the whole weekend on Bald Head Island!"

"If you're lucky," said Mr. Jamison, "you might get to meet the Gentleman Pirate,

himself—Stede Bonnet! Come on now, it's time for dinner."

The dads started back down the beach toward the house, swinging Eden higher and higher between them.

"Oh, and kids?" Dad called back over his shoulder, "If you're not lucky? You'll meet Blackbeard."

THE END

# Check It Out

Remember I said there were lots of great resources about lighthouses, pirates, maps, and the Cape Fear area? Here are some of my favorites.

- One of the most interesting books I came across was written in 1724 with the title, *A General History of the Robberies and Murders of the most notorious Pyrates*. The author is Captain Charles Johnson, but historians believe it was actually written by Daniel Defoe—the author of *Robinson Crusoe*!

This is a big book—almost 300 pages—and has information about more than 35 pirates, including Stede Bonnet and Blackbeard. It's hard to read, but I think it's cool to be reading a book that somebody wrote almost 300 years ago. And, it's still one of the best sources of information about Atlantic Coast pirates.

- I also like Miller Pope's book called, *Infamous Pirates and Their Incredible Lives*. Mr. Pope offers lots of information about lots of pirates including those that sailed around Cape Fear.

- One of my favorite lighthouse books is *Lighthouses of the Carolinas: A Short History and Guide,* by Terrance Zepke.

- The Outer Banks Lighthouse Society (OBLHS) had a rare visit to the Price's Creek Lighthouse in 2005, and Stephen Wilmoth posted an article with a great set of pictures at this link: lighthousedigest.com/Digest/StoryPage.cfm?StoryKey=2251

- The Whale Net website (administered by Wheelock College) has excellent information about satellite whale tracking that you can use to learn more or track whales on your own: whale.wheelock.edu

- The National Oceanic Atmospheric Administration (NOAA) used to be the place to get navigational charts for the U.S. Now you can find them at this link: nauticalchartsonline.com/charts/NOAA Type 11537 in the search box to see the chart for the Cape Fear to Wilmington area. Zoom in on the chart and see what you can learn about the Cape Fear River.

- Last, but not least, we had a fun and very informative trip out on the Cape Fear River with Captain Bert Felton and his wife Becky (!) aboard the *Solomon T* out of Southport. I can't begin to tell you all the things I learned, but if you get to Southport and are lucky enough to go out on the *Solomon T*, say 'hello' from me.

## By the Way

If you want to send a letter to the president of Archer-Daniel-Midland (the current owner of the Price's Creek Lighthouse) and ask them to take steps to preserve North Carolina's smallest lighthouse, you can write him at this address:

Mr. Juan R. Luciano
Archer-Daniels-Midland Corporation
77 West Wacker Drive, Suite 4600
Chicago, Illinois  60601

Coming Soon from
A&M Writing and Publishing

# The Secret on Bald Head Island

Sam, Becky, and their new friends Troy, Andrew, and L.C. are doing their best to help the ghost of Stede Bonnet claim his greatest treasure before Blackbeard finds it. When the latest clue points them toward "Old Baldy," the hunt moves to Bald Head Island on North Carolina's Cape Fear.

The only problem? It's Pirate Days on the island, and everyone is dressed...well, like a pirate. Can Sam, Becky, and their friends tell who's in costume and who's a real pirate? Join the fun in *The Secret on Bald Head Island*.

**A&M Writing and Publishing**
Santa Clara, California
www.amwriting.com

$9.95                    ISBN  978-0-9764824-9-9

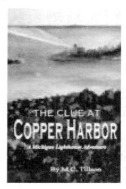